DATE DUE	

This Is the Way We Eat Our Lunch

A Book About Children Around the World

This Is the Way We Eat Our Lunch

A Book About Children Around the World

by **EDITH BAER**

Illustrated by
STEVE BJÖRKMAN

SCHOLASTIC
HARDCOVER

SCHOLASTIC • NEW YORK

To children everywhere —
wishing you good food to eat,
good friends to meet.
                              — E.B.

For Anguyo Simon,
our friend in Uganda.
                              — S.B.

Library of Congress Cataloging-in-Publication Data

Baer, Edith.
    This is the way we eat our lunch: a book about children around
the world/by Edith Baer: illustrated by Steve Björkman.
        p. cm.
    Summary: Relates in rhyme what children eat in countries
around the world.
    ISBN 0-590-46887-1
    [1. Food habits — Fiction. 2. Manners and customs — Fiction.]
I. Björkman. Steve. ill. II. Title.
PZ8.3.B137Th   1995
[E] — dc20   94-9753
                                                   CIP
                                                    AC

12 11 10 9 8 7 6 5 4 3 2 1   5 6 7 8 9/9 0/0

Printed in the USA   37

First printing, September 1995

Time for lunch! What will it be?
Come along—let's taste and see!

Massachusetts, USA

Doug eats chowder by the shore—
digs right in for clams galore!

Benjy, on a boardwalk stroll,
has a hot dog on a roll.

Pennsylvania, USA

Max and Millie, willy-nilly,
have their pretzels à la Philly.

South Carolina, USA

Merrilee can't wait to try
Mama's sweet potato pie.

Florida, USA

And Lucinda follows suit
with a lunch of luscious fruit.

Louisiana, USA

When his appetite is jumbo,
Lou has Louisiana gumbo.

Texas, USA

Just a little farther west,
Sue likes tasty tacos best.

Chip loves burgers (please, well-done!),
ketchup, pickles—picnic fun!

But the favorite lunch of Reggie's
is a burger made of—VEGGIES!

California, USA

Salads—crunchy, crisp, and green—
keep Petunia lithe and lean.

Manitoba, Canada

In the prairie winter storm,
soup makes Pete feel snug and warm.

Quebec, Canada

And Denise and Desirée
share a light-as-air soufflé.

Puerto Rico

Plantains grow in giant bunches.
Pablo likes them fried for lunches.

Fresh tamales, spicy hot!
Flora loves them—who would not?

Ghana

Amma savors beans and rice—
cooked with fish, they're twice as nice!

In Morocco and points east,
every day's a couscous feast.

Israel

Mira and Jamila spread
hummus on flat pita bread.

Italy

And Emilio Marconi
sprinkles cheese on macaroni!

England

Belinda calls Bubble and Squeak
the jolly best meal of the week,

India

while Ram, far away in Bombay,
says, "Hurry, it's curry today!"

China

Mei's chopsticks are so much fun
her dumplings are gone, one by one!

Japan

Mayumi's tempura treat
looks almost too lovely to eat!

Australia

And in Queensland, Steve and Stu have a backyard barbecue.

Time to get home! I've a hunch
we'll meet new friends for lunch!

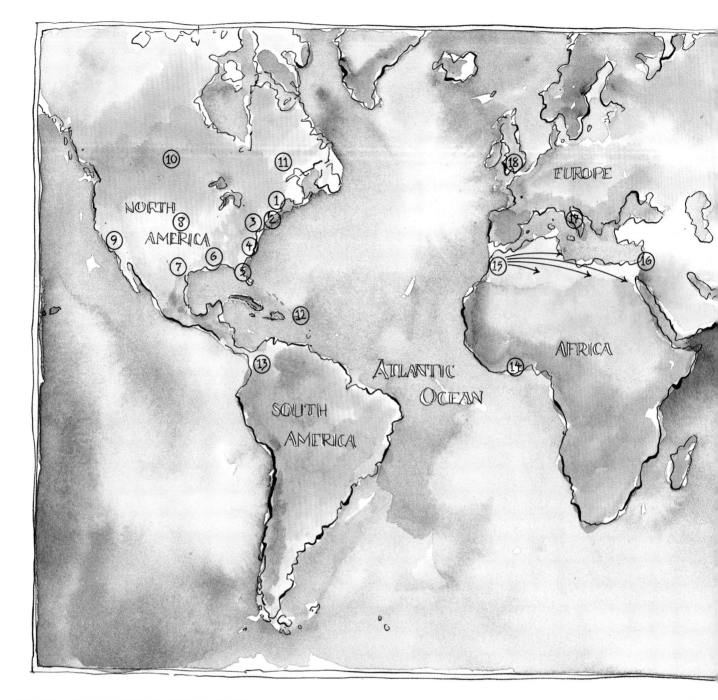

THIS IS WHERE WE LIVE

In the United States:

1. Doug lives in Massachusetts.
2. Benjy lives in Coney Island, New York, NY.
3. Max and Millie live in Philadelphia, Pennsylvania.
4. Merrilee lives in South Carolina.
5. Lucinda lives in Florida.
6. Lou lives in Louisiana.
7. Sue lives in Texas.
8. Chip and Reggie live in Kansas.
9. Petunia lives in California.

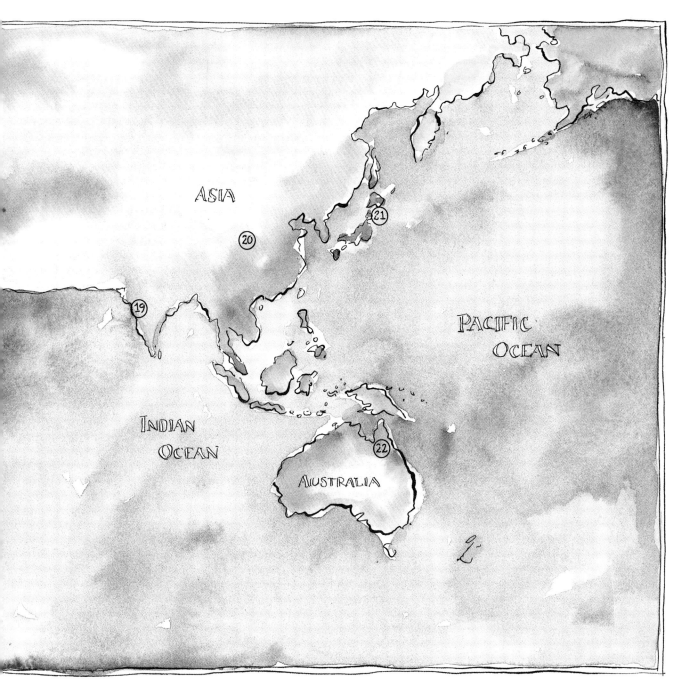

In other places around the world:

⑩ Pete lives in Manitoba, Canada.
⑪ Denise and Desirée live in Quebec, Canada.
⑫ Pablo lives in Puerto Rico.
⑬ Flora lives in Colombia.
⑭ Amma lives in Ghana.
⑮ These children are from Morocco, Algeria, Tunisia, Libya, and Egypt.

⑯ Mira and Jamila live in Israel.
⑰ Emilio lives in Italy.
⑱ Belinda lives in England.
⑲ Ram lives in India.
⑳ Mei lives in China.
㉑ Mayumi lives in Japan.
㉒ Steve and Stu live in Australia.

Recipes

Here are some recipes for you to try with a grown-up!

Lucinda's Fruit Salad

To make Lucinda's fruit salad, you will need:

1 orange, peeled and cut up; remove seeds

1/2 grapefruit, peeled and cut up; remove seeds

1 small banana, peeled and sliced

1 cup seedless grapes

1/2 cup raisins

1/2 cup orange juice

1. Mix all ingredients in a bowl and chill.
2. Serve for lunch with cottage cheese, or top with frozen yogurt or sherbet for a snack or dessert.

Hummus is a dip made from chickpeas. It is a favorite dish of children in Israel and the Middle East.

To make hummus, you will need:

1 can chickpeas, drained

2/3 cup tahini* — enough to make a smooth dip (or use 1/4 cup olive oil)

1 teaspoon salt

4 teaspoons lemon juice

2 cloves garlic

parsley, finely chopped

1. Drain the chickpeas.
2. Put the chickpeas in a food processor or blender.
3. Add the other ingredients, except the parsley. Blend well.
4. Place in a serving dish.
5. Sprinkle with the chopped parsley, and chill.
6. Spread on pita bread.

*Tahini is a paste made from sesame seeds. It is sold in markets that specialize in foods of the Middle East.

Wild Rice Soup will keep you snug and warm during the winter in Manitoba — or anywhere! Wild rice is really a grain. It was first cultivated by Native Canadian peoples long ago.

To make Wild Rice soup, you will need:

6 tablespoons butter or margarine
1 small onion, finely chopped
1/2 cup flour
3 cups chicken broth
1/2 teaspoon salt

2 cups cooked wild rice (or 1 cup each white rice and wild rice)
1 cup milk
parsley or chives, finely chopped

1. Melt the butter in a saucepan and cook the onion until tender.
2. Blend in the flour; slowly stir in the broth.
3. Stir until soup begins to boil; continue for 1 minute.
4. Stir in the salt and the rice; simmer for 5 minutes.
5. Blend in the milk and heat to serving temperature.
6. Serve in bowls or mugs and sprinkle with parsley or chives.

Did you know that...

Barbecue is a way of roasting or broiling meats, fish, chicken, or vegetables on a rack over hot coals.

Bean stew is made of black-eyed beans, fried onions, and tomatoes, and may also be cooked with pieces of smoked fish. It's usually served with rice or yams.

Bubble and Squeak is a dish of the British Isles. Mashed potatoes and cooked cabbage are shaped into a patty and fried — until you can hear a "bubble and squeak" sound coming from the skillet!

Burgers (or hamburgers) are patties of broiled ground beef named after the German city of Hamburg, where they were first served. Today they are also prepared from ground turkey or chicken. They are usually eaten on a hamburger bun or roll — with ketchup!

Chinese dumplings are small pasta pouches with cooked ground meat at the center. They're in the same pasta family as ravioli (from Italy), kreplach (a Jewish specialty from Eastern Europe), and Swabian Maultaschen (of southern Germany).

Chowder is a hearty New England stew made of clams or fish, broth, milk, potatoes, and seasonings.

Couscous is a grain that looks and tastes much like farina. In North Africa and the Middle East, steamed couscous is combined with lamb or chicken and vegetables. In Egypt, it's served with sugar and nuts!

Curry powder is a spice used widely in foods in India; a meat, fish, or rice dish seasoned with curry powder is called curry.

Hot dogs are frankfurters made of meat,

turkey, or chicken, boiled or grilled. They can be served on a roll with sauerkraut and mustard or relish for a portable lunch on the boardwalk or anywhere!

Louisiana gumbo is a Creole stew. Okra, mussels, tomatoes, chicken, or fish are cooked with onions and peppers in a spicy sauce.

Macaroni is a tube-shaped pasta — shorter, wider, and less squiggly than spaghetti. Tastes good with tomato sauce and cheese!

Plantains are large tropical fruits in the banana family. They are grown and enjoyed in Puerto Rico, the Caribbean, Latin America, and Africa. They must be cooked to become edible.

Pretzels are knot-shaped rolls brought to this country from Germany. It's the mustard on top that makes it a pretzel à la Philly!

Salads can be made of many good things. Some are made by cutting up and tossing together several kinds of vegetables — leafy green lettuces, cucumbers, peppers, radishes, cabbage, onions, and more.

Soufflé is a delicate dessert made of egg yolks and beaten egg whites and sugar. Baked in a round dish until it puffs up at the top,

it's a party treat for children in France and Quebec, Canada.

Sweet potato pie is a fluffy custard of mashed sweet potatoes, beaten eggs, and molasses baked in a flaky crust.

Tacos are fried tortillas (flat, round pieces of cornmeal or flour bread) that are folded and stuffed with a mixture of seasoned chopped meat, cheese, lettuce, tomatoes, and onions. Children have fun choosing the different ingredients to make their own tacos.

Tamales are tasty meat pies, steamed in cornhusks or banana leaves. They are eaten not only in Colombia, but in Mexico and other countries in Latin America — and they're becoming popular in the United States, too!

Tempura is a dish of Japan made of vegetables or seafood dipped in a batter and fried. It comes to the table gracefully arranged on the plate.

Veggieburgers are meatless hamburgers, made of cooked and mashed soybeans, tofu, or vegetables — mixed with grains or seeds, diced onions, peppers, and seasonings such as soy sauce. Broiled and served on a bun with ketchup, they can taste like the "real thing"!

Food is good.
Food helps us to be well and strong.
But many children in many places have very little to eat.
Could you and your friends think of ways to help,
so that children everywhere will have good food to eat?
— E.B.